A Pompey Person's

guide to
everything
GREAT
about
SOUTHAMPTON

Life is Amazing

A Life Is Amazing Paperback

A Pompey Person's Guide To
Everything Great About Southampton

First published 2016 by Life Is Amazing
ISBN: 978-0-9956394-2-3
First Edition

Introduction

Welcome to this Pompey person's guide to everything that's great about S**ton.

After exhaustive research and years of study of that other place, the author is now an expert on all things S**ton.

The great, the good, the amazing and the wonderful about the town have all been included in this handy volume. This book will break down your prejudices and reveal all the great stuff you never knew didn't exist.

If you thought S**ton was just a place where sinking liners sailed from, or the home of a feeble football team... think again.

The following pages will reveal the hidden glories of S**ton. True, they *are* so hidden that they're difficult to find, but don't let that put you off.

Take your seat, perhaps on the loo, and prepare to be amazed.

And remember, if you're out of toilet roll, this book may be a lifesaver.

All the best,

Jon O'Pompi.

So, first.

Um...

Now, I'm sure there's something...

Er...

Hold on, let me think...

I'm sure there's something...

Wait! What about..?

Er, no. I was wrong.

Nope. I give up.

Oh...

Yes...

The A27.

It takes you away from S**ton to...

...POMPEY!!